Jon Scieszka's TRUCKTOWN

Tyres for Ted

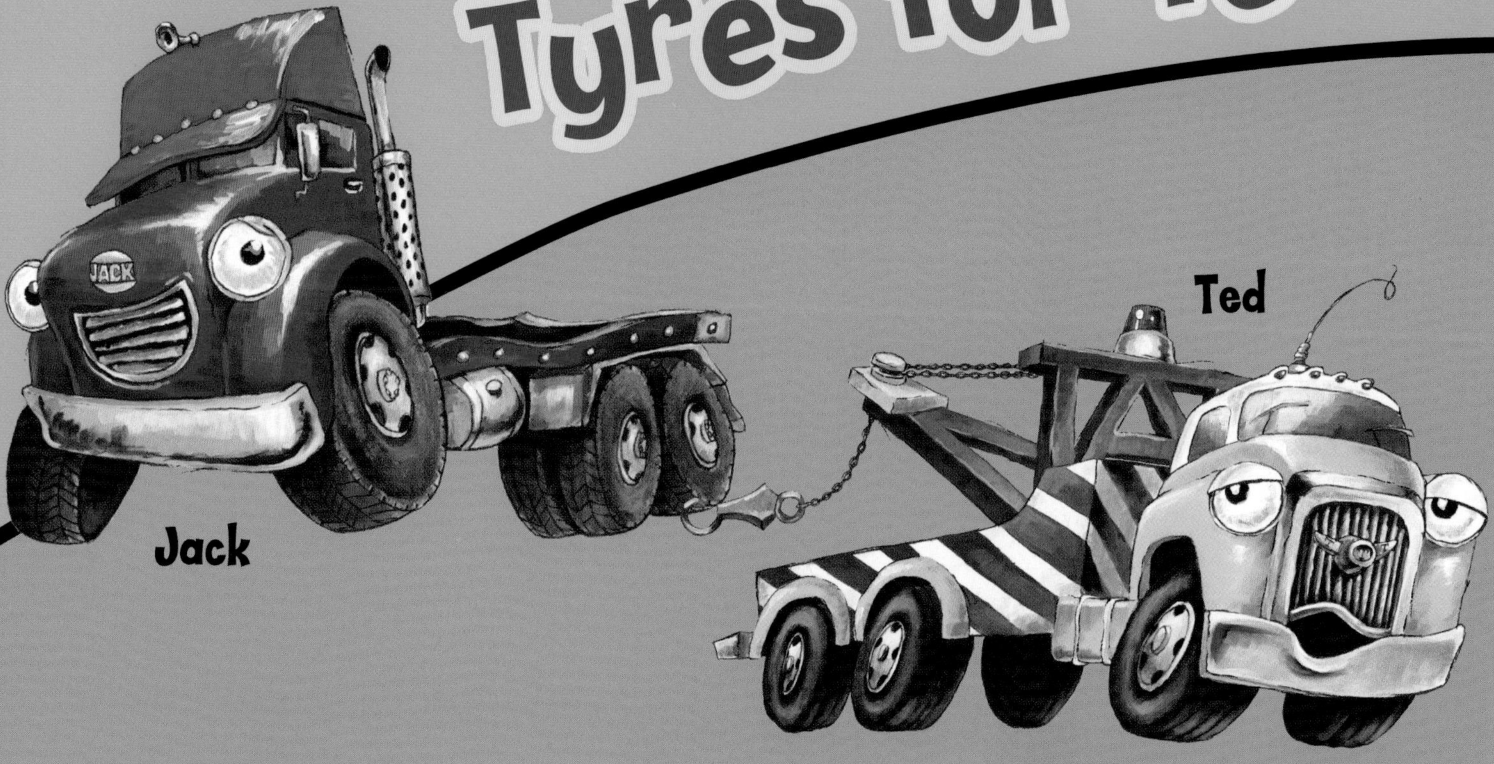

Adapted by Alison Hawes

Illustrated by Design Garage

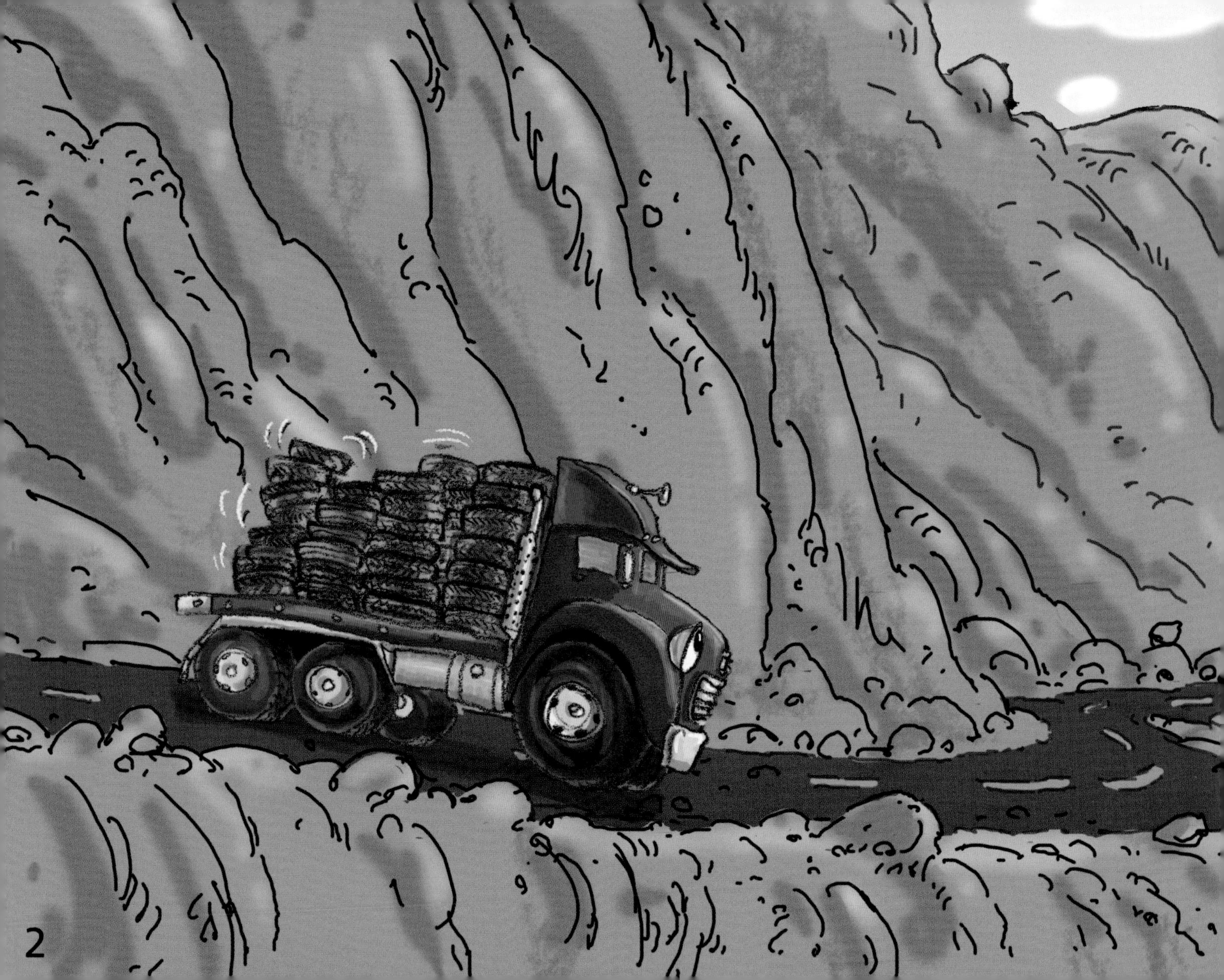

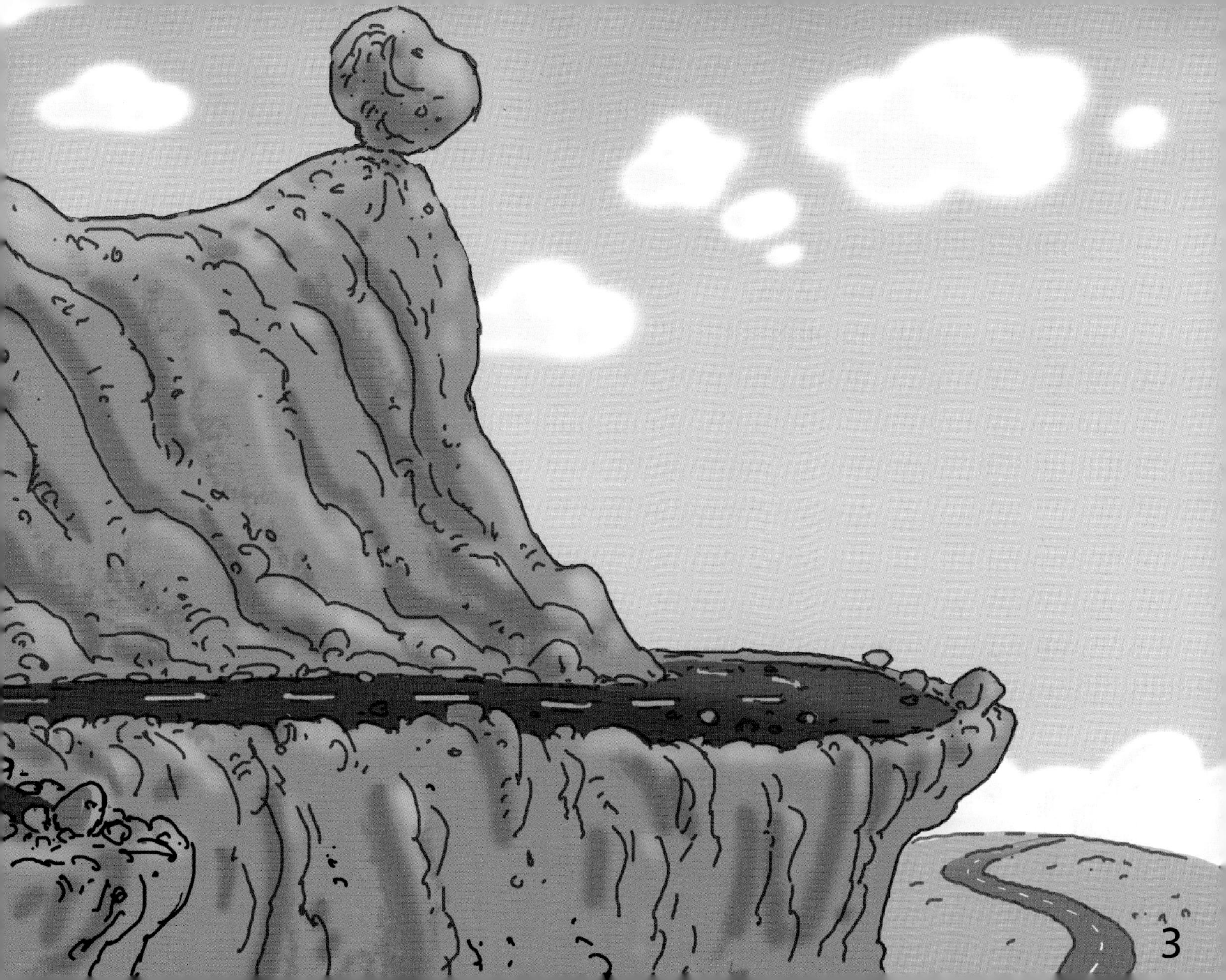

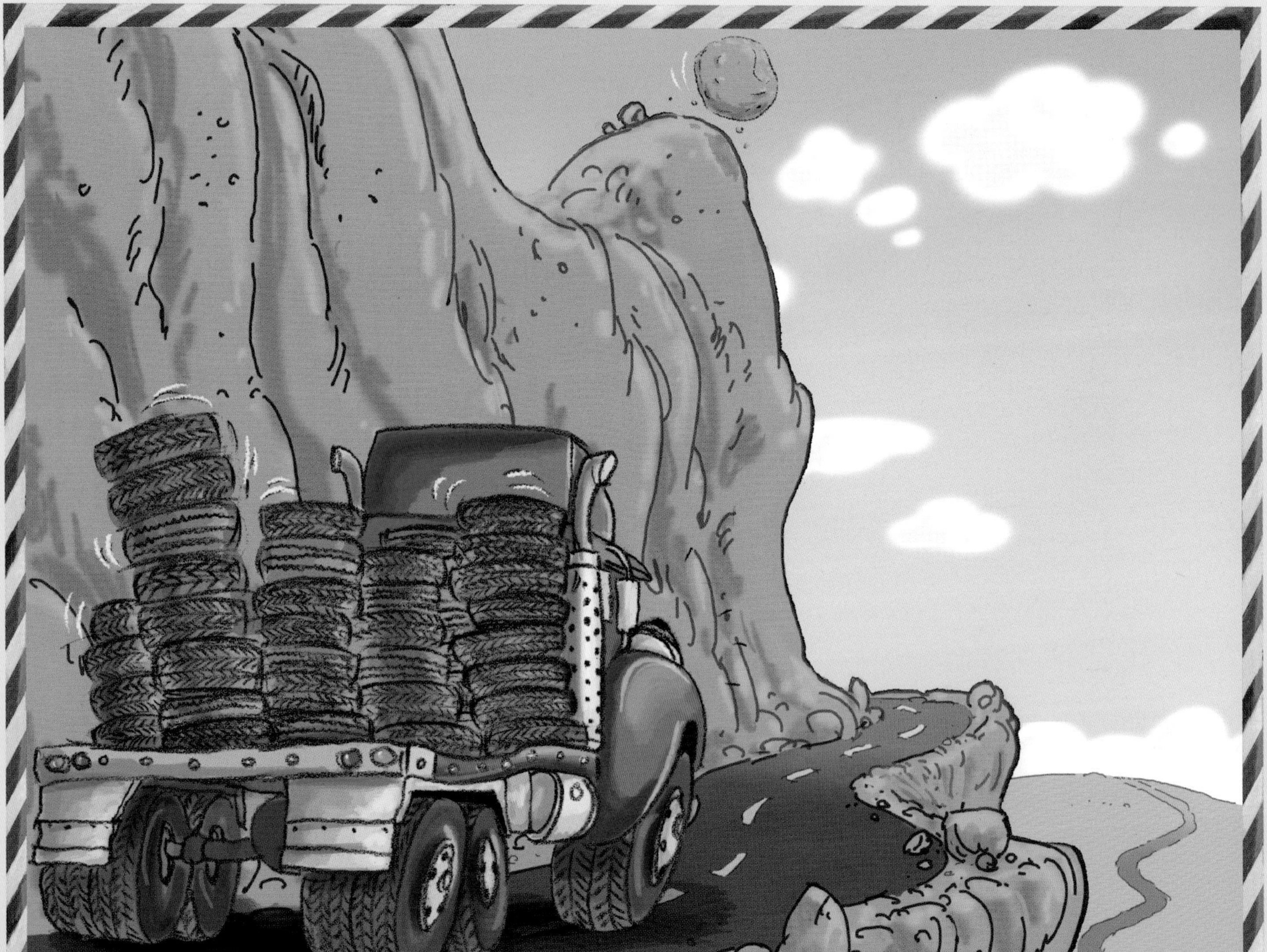

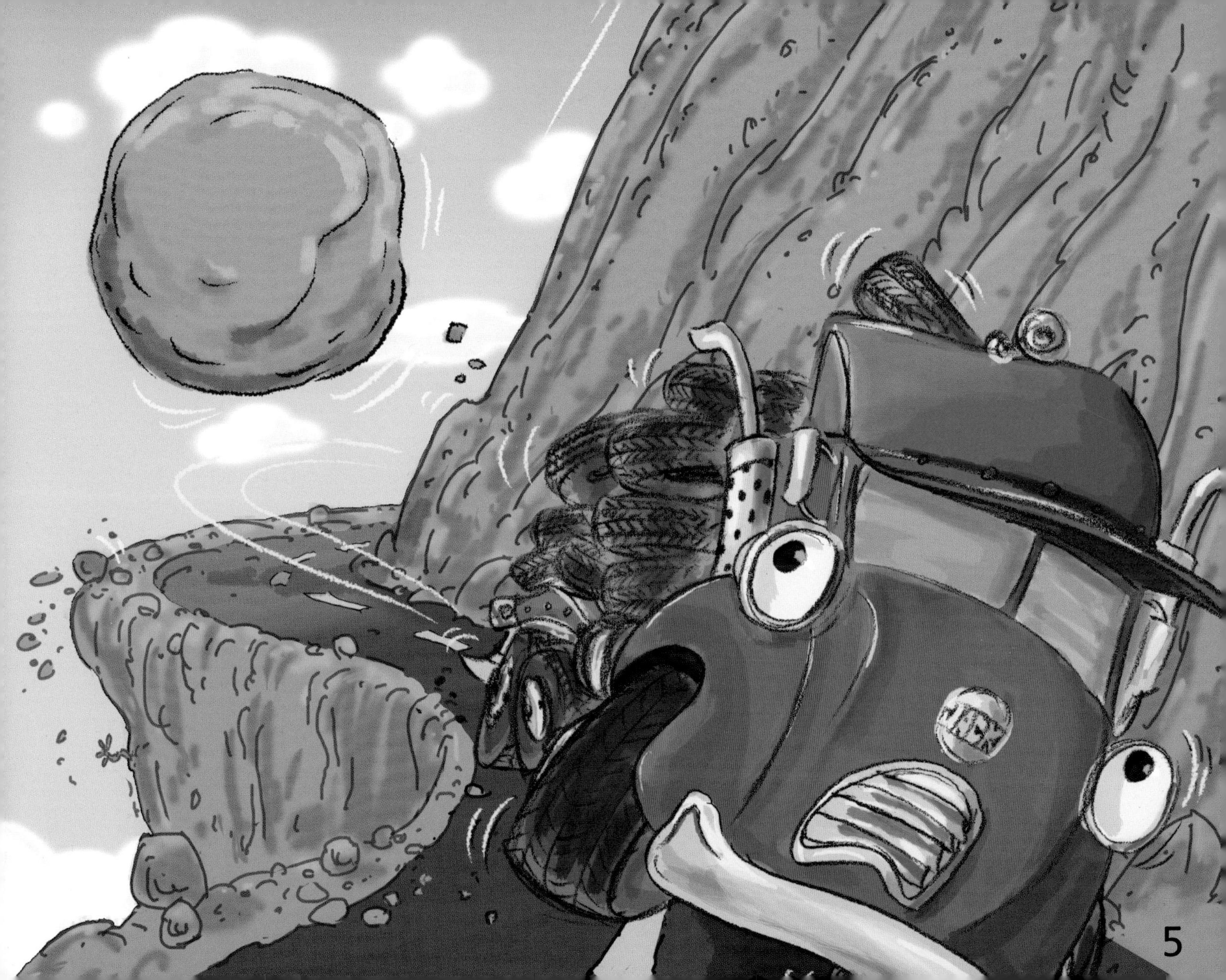

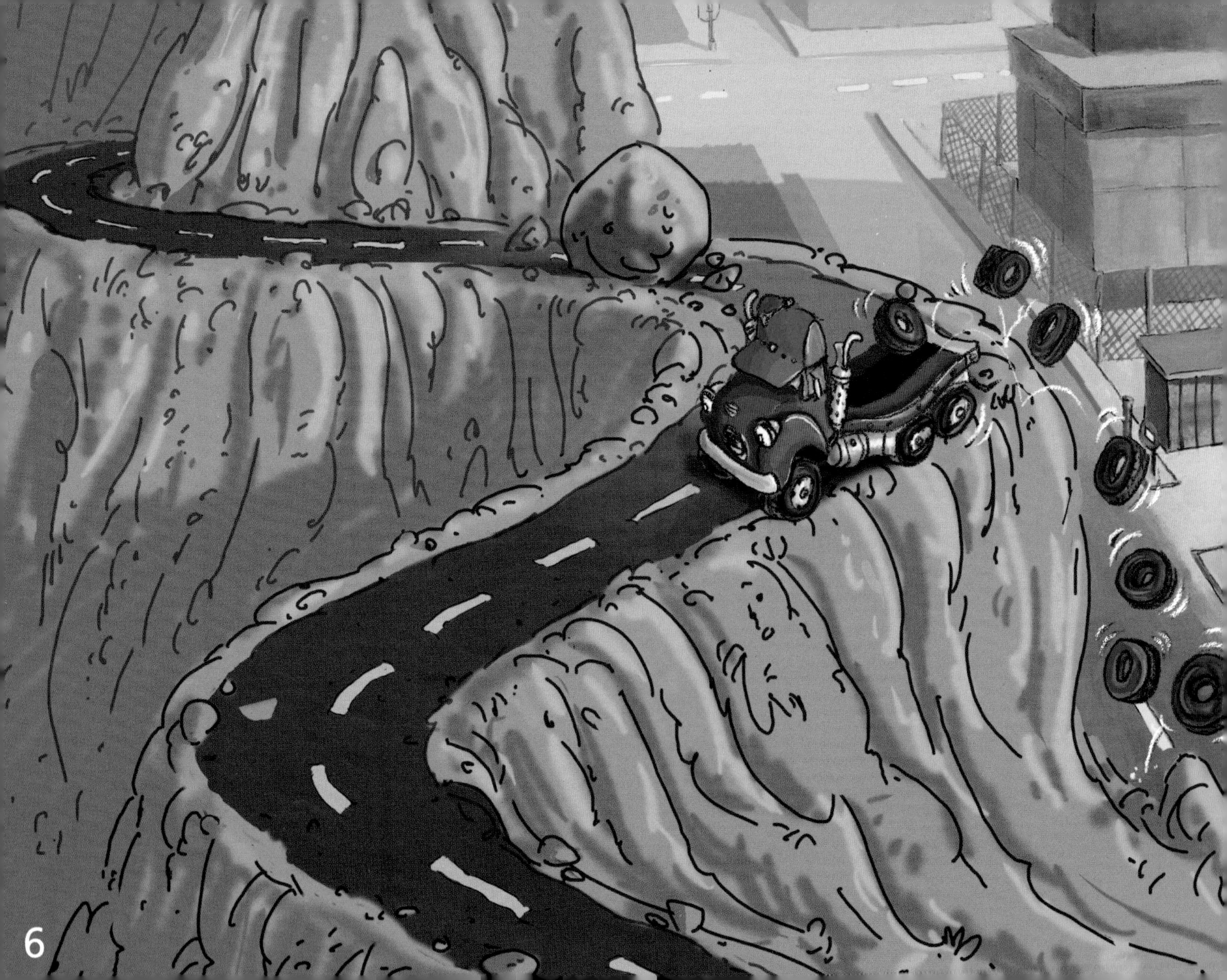

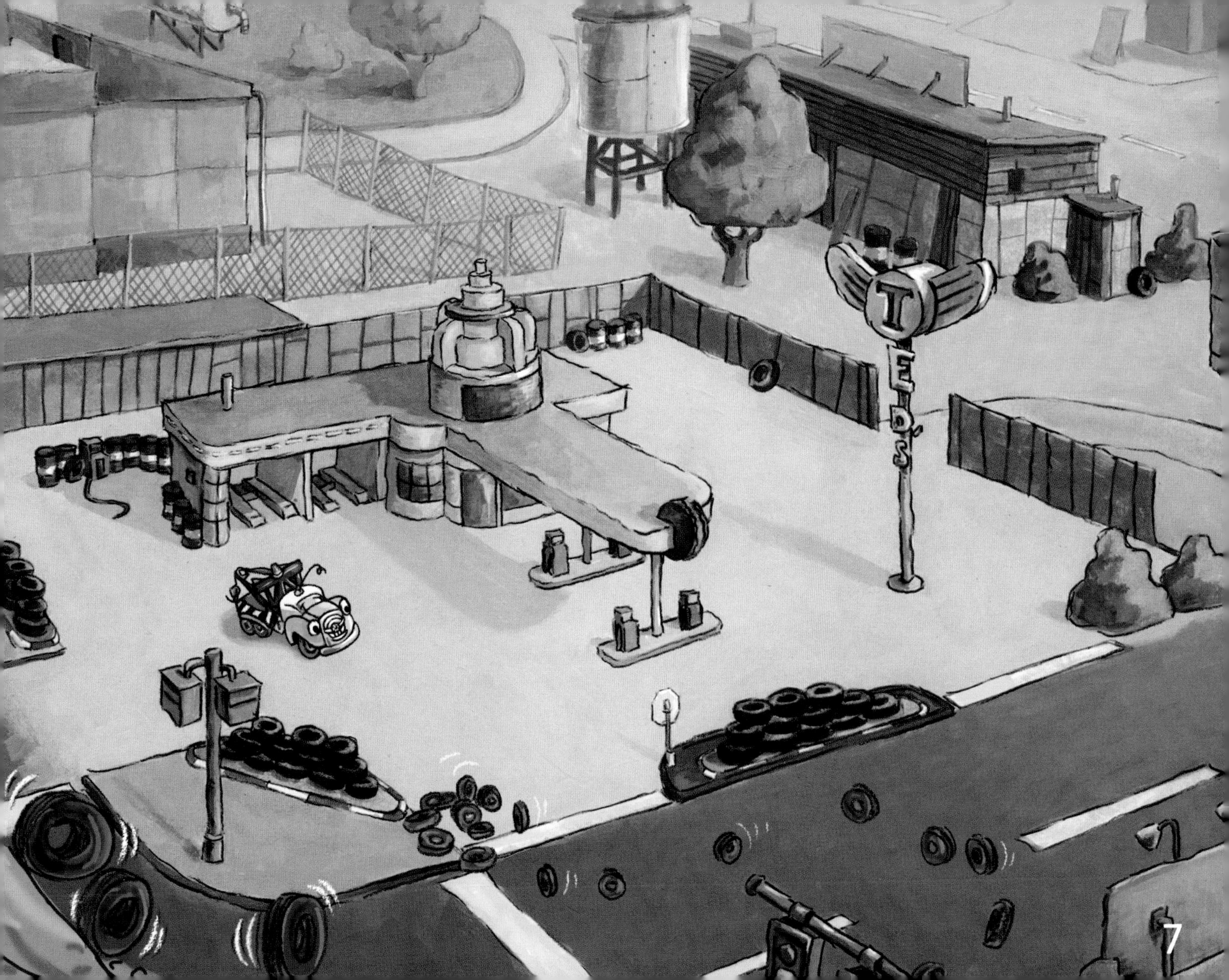
TED'S

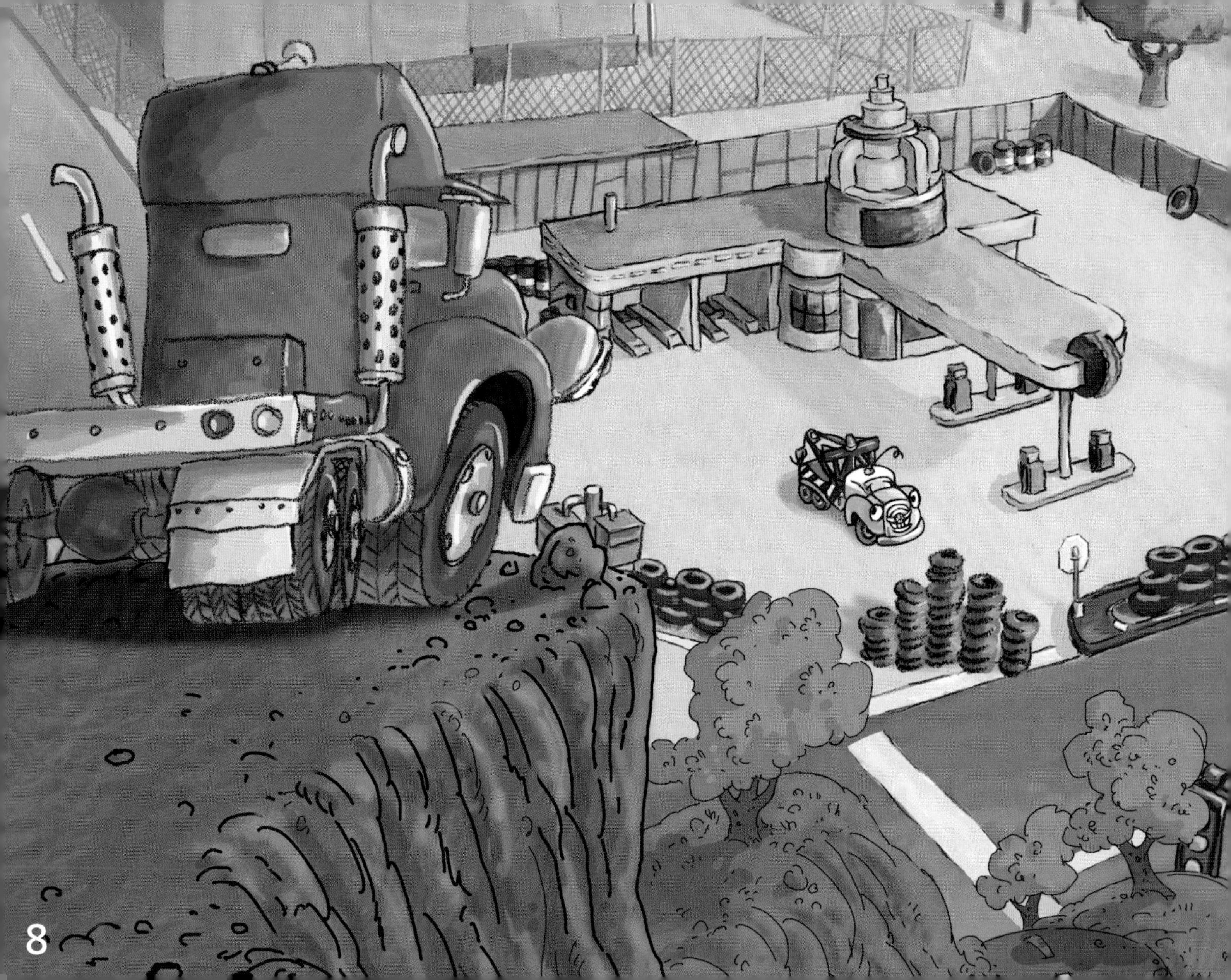